Counting Sea Life

with
the little Seahorse

Written by Sheri Fink and Derek Taylor Kent

Illustrations by Lynx Animation Studios

Books by Sheri Fink:

The Little Rose
The Little Gnome
The Little Firefly
Exploring the Garden with the Little Rose
The Little Seahorse

Books by Derek Taylor Kent:

El Perro con Sombrero
Simon and the Solar System
The *Scary School* Series
Kubrick's Game

COUNTING SEA LIFE WITH THE LITTLE SEAHORSE
By Sheri Fink and Derek Taylor Kent

Text and illustrations copyright © 2017 by Sheri Fink and Derek Taylor Kent
The *Little Seahorse* character is based on the artwork of
Mary Erikson Washam, copyright © 2014.
Adapted with permission of Mary Erikson Washam.

Library of Congress Control Number: 2017910103
ISBN: 0986446882
FIRST EDITION

It's a wonderful ocean, a magical sea!
Would you like to count
all the sea life with me?

There's one wandering whale.
Do you see it, too?

There's two tiny turtles.
I bet that you do!

There's three leafy sea dragons
feeling real flinchy.

There's four cranky crabs. Yikes!
They're trying to pinch me!

There's five hungry sharks with their
shark teeth all bared

And six bouncy blowfish that puff
when they're scared!

6

I wonder if angelfish
came here from heaven?

I don't know for sure,
but of them I count seven.

There's eight ninja narwhals and nine
squishy squids,

And ten tuna in tutus
with two tuna kids.

Eleven moray eels are hiding
deep inside a rock,

While twelve red rocking lobsters
snap their claws around the clock.

There's thirteen dandy dolphins
and fourteen silly seals

And fifteen jolly jellyfish
enjoying jelly meals.

There's sixteen shimmering shrimp
and seventeen radiant rays

And eighteen excited oysters
performing oyster plays.

Romeo and Oysterette

There's nineteen stunning starfish,
who creep among the corals.

There's twenty pirate pipefish and thirty blushing bubbles!

It's a wonderful ocean, a magical sea.
I'm happy you counted
the sea life with me!

There's just one more thing that I
think we should do …

Come in for a photo, all the creatures
and YOU!